We Need
Garbage Collectors

by Lisa Trumbauer

Consulting Editor: Gail Saunders-Smith, Ph.D.

Consultant: James V. Biamonte, President
New York State Association
for Solid Waste Management

Pebble Books

an imprint of Capstone Press
Mankato, Minnesota

Pebble Books are published by Capstone Press
151 Good Counsel Drive, P.O. Box 669, Mankato, Minnesota 56002
http://www.capstone-press.com

1 2 3 4 5 6 08 07 06 05 04 03

Library of Congress Cataloging-in-Publication Data
Trumbauer, Lisa, 1963–
    We need garbage collectors / by Lisa Trumbauer.
        p. cm.—(Helpers in our community)
    Summary: Simple text and photographs present garbage collectors and their
role in the community.
    Includes bibliographical references and index.
    ISBN 0-7368-1650-X (hardcover)
    1. Refuse collectors—Juvenile literature. 2. Refuse and refuse disposal—
Juvenile literature. [1. Refuse collectors. 2. Refuse and refuse disposal.
3. Occupations.] I. Title. II. Series.
HD8039.R46T78 2003
363.72′85′023—dc21   2002007663

Note to Parents and Teachers

The Helpers in Our Community series supports national social
studies standards for units related to community helpers and
their roles. This book describes and illustrates garbage collectors
and how they help communities stay clean. The photographs
support early readers in understanding the text. This book also
introduces early readers to subject-specific vocabulary words, which
are defined in the Words to Know section. Early readers may need
assistance to read some words and to use the Table of Contents,
Words to Know, Read More, Internet Sites, and Index/Word List
sections of the book.

DEC   2005

Table of Contents

Garbage collectors help keep our communities clean.

Garbage collectors
work in cities and
in the country.

Garbage collectors
drive garbage trucks.

Garbage collectors
pick up garbage at homes
and at businesses.

Garbage collectors empty garbage cans into their trucks.

Some garbage collectors empty their trucks into a landfill.

Many garbage collectors collect items for recycling.

They empty their trucks
at a recycling plant.
They recycle plastic,
newspapers, and glass.

Garbage collectors
are important helpers
in our community.

Words to Know

business—a place where people work

collect—to gather something; garbage collectors collect garbage from homes and businesses.

garbage—most of the items that people throw away; old food, packaging, old toys, and broken items are often thrown away as garbage.

landfill—a place where garbage is dumped and then buried; the garbage is buried between layers of soil to protect the earth and the water supply.

recycle—the process of turning something old into something new; recycling allows people to use items again; soda cans, some plastic items, newspapers, and cardboard are often recycled.

recycling plant—a building where old things are taken first before being turned into new things

Read More

Bryant-Mole, Karen. *You're a Community Helper.* Pretend. Des Plaines, Ill.: Heinemann Interactive Library, 1998.

Deedrick, Tami. *Garbage Collectors.* Community Helpers. Mankato, Minn.: Bridgestone Books, 1998.

MacGregor, Cynthia. *Recycling a Can.* The Rosen Publishing Group's Reading Room Collection. New York: Rosen Publishing Group, 2003.

Internet Sites

Track down many sites about garbage and recycling. Visit the FACT HOUND at *http://www.facthound.com*

IT IS EASY! IT IS FUN!

1) Go to *http://www.facthound.com*

2) Type in: 073681650X

3) Click on "FETCH IT" and FACT HOUND will find several links hand-picked by our editors.

Relax and let our pal FACT HOUND do the research for you!

Index/Word List

Word Count: 77
Early-Intervention Level: 9

Editorial Credits
Mari C. Schuh, editor; Abby Bradford, Bradfordesign, Inc., series designer; Molly Nei, book designer; Karrey Tweten, photo researcher

Photo Credits
Bruce Coleman Inc./Phil Degginger, 18
Capstone Press/Jim Foell, cover, 6, 8
Corbis/David H. Wells, 12; Martyn Goddard, 14; Kevin R. Morris, 20
Folio, Inc./Art Stein, 4
Index Stock Imagery/Stewart Cohen, 1
Unicorn Stock Photos/Eric R. Berndt, 10; Dick Young, 16